sesame workshop™

Grover Stays Up Very, Very Late

Written by Susan Rich Brooke
Illustrated by Tom Brannon
Original music composed by Curtis Marolt

Read along as I tell you a very interesting story about my very late night. You will know it is time to turn the page when you hear this sound.... Okay, here it is!

publications international, ltd.

Hello, everybodee! This is your old pal, Grover. I am in bed.
It is nighttime, and I am wearing my jammies. So, I bet you
think I am going to sleep. But I am not. I, Grover, am going
to stay up very, very late.

If you want to know why, you have to turn the page.
No, not yet! Do you not remember? Wait for the sound.
I know you can do it. It is not this sound   or this
one.   But get ready. The next sound will mean it is
time to turn the page. Here it comes....

2

3

Oh! Hello again!

Now I will tell you why I am going to stay up very, very late. I want to know what my Mommy does after I go to sleep. And the only way I can find out is to stay awake.

There is only one teensy problem. I do not know how to stay awake past my bedtime.

I think I will set my alarm clock, just in case I fall asleep. But do not worry, I will not! And in case you were wondering, I will not fall asleep on the next page either.

6

Zzzz. Ah ha ha! Just kidding! I, Grover, am still wide awake. I cannot possibly fall asleep, because I cannot stop thinking about what my Mommy does when it is very, very late.

Hmmm. I wonder if she will be at a big party, eating chocolate cake and playing pin the tail on the monster. That is my favorite game! Mommy and I always play it together.

8

It is late. But it is not very, very late. I think I will take a little nap. No! I cannot take a nap! If I take a nap, I will be asleep. And if I am asleep, then I will not be awake.

Hmmm. Here is what I am going to do. I am going to read my favorite book. Ahem.

"Once upon a time, there were twelve sleeping princesses. Every night, the princesses fell fast asleep. One princess fell asleep. Two princesses fell asleep. Three princesses . . ."

Huh? Oh no! That is my favorite story for falling asleep, not for staying awake.

Just as soon as it is very, very late, I will creep down the stairs and see what Mommy is doing. Maybe she will be watching a movie and eating popcorn. I love watching movies with Mommy. And I love sharing popcorn with Mommy! I better stay awake so Mommy will not have to eat all that popcorn by herself.

It is very late. But it is not very, very late. Hmmm. Staying awake is harder than I thought.

Whenever I have trouble falling asleep, I count something quiet, like sheep. So tonight I will count something noisy, like monkeys! If you count with me, you can stay awake too. Are you ready?

One monkey whistling. Two monkeys tap dancing. Three monkeys tickling. Four monkeys snoring. Zzzz ...

What was that noise? Oh, it was you turning the page. Thank you very much. You kept me from falling asleep.

If I fell asleep, I would miss all the fun things my mommy does. I wonder if she will be playing baseball. When she slides into home plate everybody will cheer. Mommy will need me there to cheer for her too! Yea, Mommy! All I have to do is stay up just a little bit later. Maybe just until the next page!

Well, it is a little bit later now. But it is not very, very late yet. And I, Grover, am getting sleepy.

How will I stay awake? I know! I will do some exercises. If you do them with me, you will stay awake too. First we will do some knee bends: 1, 2, 3, 4! Now some jumping jacks: 5, 6, 7, 8! Now some push-ups: 9, 10, 11, 12!

Ugh! My arms and legs are getting tired. But I, Grover, am wide awake!

Very, very soon I will be able to find out what Mommy does when it is very, very late. I wonder if she will be at a circus. Wowee! I love the circus! There will be jugglers juggling and clowns clowning and unicyclists, um, unicycling. Maybe Mommy will swing from a trapeze. She will need me to swing along beside her! And in just one little minute — oh, it is almost time for you to turn the page.

19

Whew, you are just in time. I did it! I stayed up very, very late. And if you are still reading this — which I hope you are because if you are not then I am talking to myself — then you stayed up very, very late too. Now we can both see what Mommy does when we are usually asleep.

I am tiptoeing quietly out of my room. What? It is time for you to turn the page again? Okay. Just remember to do it quietly.

20

Hello there. Thank you for turning the page so quietly. Now I am just going to take a look, and — how strange!

Where is the party? And where is the movie? And where is the baseball game? And where is the circus?

Mommy is just *sleeping*! You know, now that it is very, very late, that seems like a very, very good idea.

23

Uh, since Mommy is sleeping, I will crawl back into bed and take a little nap myself. I will see you in the morning. Not too early. Usually I, Grover, wake up very early. But tomorrow I think I am going to sleep very, very late.

Night, night everybodee.